SEVEN WONDERS
OF THE
ANCIENT WORLD

SEVEN
WONDERS
OF THE
ANCIENT
WORLD

LYNN CURLEE

ATHENEUM BOOKS FOR YOUNG READERS
New York London Toronto Sydney Singapore

THE ANCIENT HELLENISTIC WORLD

I HAVE GAZED ON THE WALLS OF IMPREGNABLE BABYLON, ALONG
WHICH CHARIOTS MAY RACE, AND ON THE ZEUS BY THE BANKS OF THE
ALPHAEUS. I HAVE SEEN THE HANGING GARDENS AND THE COLOSSUS
OF HELIOS, THE GREAT MAN-MADE MOUNTAINS OF THE LOFTY
PYRAMIDS, AND THE GIGANTIC TOMB OF MAUSOLUS. BUT WHEN I SAW
THE SACRED HOUSE OF ARTEMIS THAT TOWERS TO THE CLOUDS, THE
OTHERS WERE PLACED IN THE SHADE, FOR THE SUN HIMSELF HAS
NEVER LOOKED UPON ITS EQUAL OUTSIDE OLYMPUS.
—ANTIPATER OF SIDON

More than two thousand years ago, about 150 B.C., a Greek poet named Antipater of Sidon wrote a short poem naming seven wondrous marvels he had seen during his travels throughout the eastern Mediterranean world. Seven was a mystical number to ancient people, and each of these spectacular sights was a masterpiece of architecture, sculpture, or engineering, famous for its great size, beauty, grandeur, and perfection.

Antipater lived during the Hellenistic age, an era when the culture of the ancient Greeks had spread throughout the Mediterranean, but before the rise of the Roman Empire, another ancient civilization that made wondrous marvels of its own. His poem is not the only list of seven wonders that has survived, but it is the earliest that we have. It was written in a time when the many splendors of Greece, Egypt, Persia, and Babylon had become tourist shrines for ancient people, like the U.S. Capitol or Mount Rushmore are today.

The ancient world ended with the fall of the Roman Empire, and for more than a millennium, the idea that seven great monuments could represent the height of human achievement was kept alive only in the almost forgotten words of the Greek writers. During those centuries most of the ancient monuments were toppled by earthquakes and buried by floods, were carted away and broken up for their precious raw materials, or simply crumbled into dust.

By about A.D. 1500 , the Renaissance in Europe was marked by a new interest in the ancient classical world. Antipater's poem was rediscovered, along with other authors' detailed descriptions of the famous monuments. But not every writer described the same seven wonders. While Antipater named the massive walls of the city of Babylon, others wrote of the Pharos, the towering lighthouse at Alexandria. Roman writers included Roman monuments. Then, in the midsixteenth century A.D., about 1,700 years after Antipater's poem was written, a Dutch artist, Maerten van

Heemskerck, made a series of engravings of the seven legendary monuments. He had no way of knowing what the ancient structures were really like, so he used his imagination and invented his own versions of them. After these engravings appeared, the list of the Seven Wonders of the Ancient World was fixed. From the oldest to the most recent, they are:

the Great Pyramid at Giza

the Hanging Gardens of Babylon

the Temple of Artemis at Ephesus

the Statue of Zeus at Olympia

the Mausoleum at Halicarnassus

the Colossus of Rhodes

the Pharos at Alexandria.

Surprisingly, all seven monuments stood complete in all their glory at the same moment in history for only a short time. The Colossus of Rhodes fell in an earthquake in 226 B.C., only about thirty years after the completion of the Pharos. At that date the Great Pyramid had already been standing for more than 2,300 years, yet only it has survived into modern times. The other wonders disappeared long ago.

But today, nearly five hundred years after van Heemskerck's imaginative engravings, we know a great deal about the Seven Wonders of the Ancient World, and the ancient civilizations that made them. In the past one hundred and fifty years, archaeologists have excavated most of their sites, and by comparing what they found to the descriptions in the old writings, a fairly good picture has emerged of how these remarkable structures actually looked. Now we have a basic understanding of why and how the human beings of the ancient world built such magnificent structures—monuments so grand that today we still regard them with amazement and awe: Seven Wonders of the Ancient World.

COLOSSUS OF RHODES

Based on M. Van Heemskerck's midsixteenth century engraving

THE GREAT PYRAMID AT GIZA

The civilization of ancient Egypt was already 3,000 years old at the time of Antipater of Sidon. To the poet, the age of the pyramids was as remote as the Hellenistic age is to us. Standing with its gigantic companion pyramids for 4,500 years on a desert plateau overlooking the river Nile at Giza, the Great Pyramid is the only one of the Seven Wonders that has survived to the present day. Visited by both Julius Caesar in Roman times and Napoléon in the late 1700s, it has always been the most famous monument on earth. Until the late nineteenth century it was the tallest structure ever built. It is also one of the largest, most massive, most stupendous objects ever made by man. Even more amazing, the technique of building with cut stone was invented by the Egyptians only about 100 years before it was constructed.

Essentially an immense artificial mountain, the Great Pyramid is a huge pile of carefully cut and fitted stones with a few small internal chambers and passages. It was built as a tomb for the pharaoh Khufu—called Cheops by the Greeks—during the years around 2580 B.C. Much more than just a king, the Egyptian pharaoh was also the link between gods and men. His role was to perform the rituals and act out the ceremonies that insured that the sun would rise and the river Nile would flow. And when he died, he became a god. The rituals surrounding his burial were the most important of all. His body was preserved as a mummy, and he was sealed in the stone tomb that was to be his palace for eternity. If all were done properly, his soul would live forever and Egypt would prosper.

During the age of the pyramids, the most important task of any pharaoh's reign was the construction of his tomb. According to tradition, it took one hundred thousand men thirty years to build the Great Pyramid. Ten years were spent in planning the project, preparing the site, building roads, quarrying stones, and constructing quarters for the workmen. Actually building the Great Pyramid took

twenty years. Modern computer models confirm that these figures could be accurate. The architects and engineers were members of the pharaoh's court. The workmen were mainly peasants and farmers who willingly became pyramid builders every year for a few months during the annual floods of the Nile. The continuing well-being of Egypt depended on the proper burial of the king.

Using only soft copper and bronze metal tools, wooden sledges, ropes and rollers to transport stones, and levers to move them about, teams of workmen built a structure 481 feet tall, the height of a fifty-story building, and almost two-thirds of a mile around at the base. It has been estimated that the Great Pyramid contains two million three hundred thousand cut-stone blocks, each weighing between two and fifteen tons—enough for a wall ten feet high around the entire country of France. Many archaeologists think that ramps of sun-dried brick were built encircling the Great Pyramid as it was rising so that the stones could be dragged up on sledges. Others propose a straight ramp that was built ever taller as it rose. A recent theory suggests that wooden rocking cradles were used with levers and wedges to raise the stones. No one knows exactly how it was done. But we do know that it was done with incredible precision. The Great Pyramid is a perfect geometrical form perfectly aligned with the compass. It was as finely made as a jewel, but on an almost inhumanly vast scale.

Today the Great Pyramid is missing its outer facing, a smooth layer of white limestone that made it gleam like a polished crystal, as well as its shining capstone, a small pyramid covered with electrum, an alloy of silver and gold. It was magnificent. How it must have astonished the people who built it!

Although his tomb was looted centuries ago by grave-robbers and now stands empty, Khufu has found a kind of immortality. This king who ruled at the dawn of human history will always be known as one of the greatest builders of all time. The Great Pyramid is not only a wonder of the ancient world, it is one of the most breathtaking wonders of mankind.

THE HANGING GARDENS OF BABYLON

Two millennia after the age of the pyramids, the largest city in the world was located on the river Euphrates in the fertile crescent of Mesopotamia. Babylon was the splendid capital of a dynasty of warrior-kings who were also great builders. It was famed especially for three spectacular structures. The ziggurat, an immense, stepped tower about three hundred feet high, loomed over the city. It was the temple of Marduk, the official state god. The massive city walls, more than ten miles around and perhaps fifty feet high, were wide enough at the top for two four-horse chariots to pass. Eight fortified ceremonial gateways provided access to the city's processional avenues. These walls were unique in all the world. The third structure was the fabled Hanging Gardens.

Ancient Greek writers tell us that the gardens were built by King Nebuchadrezzar II, who reigned in the early sixth century B.C., as a love-gift for his wife, Amytis. According to legend, she was a Persian princess who longed for the cool, wooded mountains of her childhood. The king made for her a vast private park full of large trees and exotic plants of every description, with cool glades and bubbling streams and fountains. It was built high off the ground, within the palace walls, on a series of lofty stone terraces to resemble mountain scenery. From a distance the gardens must have seemed to float or hang over the city walls of hot, dry, dusty Babylon like a beautiful mirage.

Babylon was built almost completely of sun-dried brick. Vast armies of laborers spent their lives making millions of bricks by hand. But brick is not as durable as stone. Unlike the everlasting pyramids, the monumental buildings of ancient Babylon crumbled into shapeless piles of rubble long ago. In the early twentieth century archaeologists uncovered the foundations of the ziggurat, and found the boundaries of the city walls, but for years they could not discover the site

of the Hanging Gardens. Then one day the foundations of a strange building were excavated within the walls of Nebuchadrezzar's palace. It had fourteen stone chambers arranged as though providing support for a great weight, such as what thousands of tons of soil and enormous trees would need. Stonework was rare in the brick buildings of Babylon, and the Hanging Gardens is one of the places where we are told it was used. In addition, there was evidence of an unusual well that could have been built for a slave-powered waterwheel machine to constantly irrigate the park. It is possible that the Hanging Gardens have been found.

But not all experts agree. The same ancient writers who say that the gardens were made of stone tell us that they were located close by the Euphrates, while the stone ruins are far from the river. Several different sites have been proposed, and there are even those who believe that the Hanging Gardens were a myth. They base their argument on the fact that only Greek writers have described the gardens. It certainly does seem strange that even though the Babylonian kings left extensive records bragging of their other building campaigns, no mention has ever been found of the famous gardens in the Babylonian inscriptions themselves.

So today the Hanging Gardens of Babylon remain a tantalizing mystery. Babylon is six hundred miles from the Mediterranean—far from the center of the Hellenistic world. It is possible that the Greek writers blended fact and fiction. Eyewitness accounts were easily mixed up with legends in the ancient world, just as they are today. Perhaps the steps of the ziggurat of Marduk were planted with trees. Perhaps there were many rooftop gardens in Babylon. Perhaps the fabulous Hanging Gardens actually did provide cool shade for Nebuchadrezzar and his wife. Perhaps one day we will discover the answer. Or perhaps we will never know.

THE TEMPLE OF ARTEMIS AT EPHESUS

Ephesus was one of the richest cities of the ancient world. Located in Asia Minor, where the cultures of the Near East mixed with Greek civilization, it was an important center of trade. Ephesus was conquered by King Croesus of Lydia in 560 B.C. Fabulously wealthy, Croesus admired Greek art and architecture. He built a magnificent sanctuary dedicated to Artemis, Greek goddess of the hunt. It was constructed on a site sacred to the ancient Mother-Earth goddess of the Near East, and the identities of these two goddesses became fused.

Located at the edge of the city in a spacious park, the temple of Artemis was one of the largest of all Greek temples. The temple of Zeus at Olympia had a single row of columns around the outside. The columns were about thirty feet tall. But around the temple of Artemis were two rows of lofty stone columns sixty feet high—127 in all. Approaching the building was like entering a forest of columns. Besides its great scale, the temple was lavishly decorated with sculpture that was brightly painted and gilded. In ancient Greece, temples served also as the banking centers of their cities. Much of the wealth of Ephesus was concentrated in the treasury of the temple. The enormous structure was known as the greatest, most beautiful, and most noble sanctuary in all the world.

In 356 B.C., it was all destroyed. The beautiful temple of Artemis was set afire by a madman. The fire quickly spread throughout the wooden parts of the structure—the gilded doors, the stairways that led to the roof, and the massive beams that supported it. It was an act of desecration that horrified the civilized world. The arsonist claimed that he did it because he wanted his name to be remembered. It has been. It was Herostratus. But in the smoking ruins of the great temple, the Ephesians found the sacred statue of Artemis unharmed. Taking this miracle as a sign from the goddess, they vowed to rebuild their sanctuary grander and even more beautiful than before.

After the debris from the fire was cleared away, a new foundation was built on top of the old one, and over a period of decades a magnificent new marble temple rose in the same spot. This time the roof supports and stairways were made of stone, and the doors were of bronze. The new temple of Artemis was the same size and almost a copy of the old one, but now the décor was even more splendid, and was done in the latest style.

Ephesus remained prosperous, and for five hundred years the beautiful new temple retained its reputation as one of the greatest sights in the ancient world. During the age of the Roman Empire, Ephesus became a Roman city, and the temple of Artemis became the temple of Diana, Roman goddess of the hunt. Then, in A.D. 262, Ephesus was invaded by the Goths, marauding tribes from the north. The temple was plundered, and its treasury raided. Gradually, over the centuries, the ruins of the great temple were broken up for building stones, the site was flooded, and the foundations sank into the swampy earth. Eventually, no one even knew where the enormous temple had stood. In the 1860s, archaeologists began to search for the remains of the temple of Artemis. The foundations were discovered under twenty feet of mud and earth. Excavations are still ongoing at Ephesus today.

According to legend, on the night when Herostratus burned Croesus's temple of Artemis, a baby was born who would conquer the world. This child would grow up to be Alexander the Great, whose conquests would spread Greek civilization all over the known world, and mark the beginning of the Hellenistic age.

THE STATUE OF ZEUS AT OLYMPIA

During the middle centuries of the first millennium B.C., the ancient Greek world was a collection of small, fiercely independent city-states united only by language, religion, and geography. Every four years, however, the Greeks joined together at the shrine of Olympia, by the river Alpheus, to honor the greatest of their gods, Zeus the Thunderer, Father and King of gods and men. Olympia was not a city, but a sanctuary, and the worship of Zeus was centered around a series of athletic contests: the Olympic Games. Victory in the games guaranteed worldwide honor and fame, and the Greeks even counted time in olympiads, the four-year interval between games.

In the year 456 B.C., a beautiful new gleaming white stone temple was dedicated to Zeus in the sacred grove at Olympia. Greek temples were built to house and protect the sacred statues of their gods. The grandest temple of the king of the gods deserved to have the most magnificent statue ever made. The job was given to Phidias of Athens, the greatest sculptor of the age.

Pausanias, a Greek writer of the second century A.D., has given us a vivid description of the incredible statue. It was not carved of stone or cast in metal, but was made of rare precious materials. The skin of the god was sculpted in panels of carved elephant ivory joined together, and the folds of his robe were made of beaten plates of solid gold. Zeus's elaborate throne was constructed of cedar wood inlaid with ebony, ivory, gold, and precious stones. The throne and the stone base on which it sat were adorned with sculpted figures illustrating scenes from Greek mythology. The thousands of individual parts were assembled on an immense wooden framework to form a seated figure more than forty feet high. Pausanias writes:

On his head lies a sculpted wreath of olive sprays. On his right hand he holds a figure of Victory made from ivory and gold. In his left hand the god holds his sceptre inlaid with every kind of metal, and the bird perched on the

sceptre is an eagle. The sandals of the god are made of gold, as is his robe, and his garments are carved with animals and with lily flowers. All the floor in front of the statue is paved with black marble, edged in a semicircle by a raised rim of Parian marble, which acts as a basin for olive oil.

When the image was completely finished, Phidias prayed to Zeus to show by a sign whether the work was to his liking. Immediately, a thunderbolt struck the spot where to this day a bronze jar stands to cover the place.

In the dim interior of the temple, lit only by flaming braziers, the spectacular glittering image of Zeus must have been overwhelming. The translucent ivory seemed to breathe with life, and the fabulous display of gold and other precious materials was simply staggering. It is no wonder that for eight hundred years pilgrims flocked to Olympia to see the most famous statue in the world.

But in the fourth century A.D., Roman Emperor Theodosius I, who was a Christian, banned the worship of the pagan gods, and the huge statue was taken as a trophy to Constantinople, capital of the Eastern Roman Empire. It was destroyed there in a fire in A.D. 462. Eventually the site of Olympia itself was leveled by earthquakes and landslides and buried by floods.

In modern times we have seen the revival of the Olympic Games. Olympia itself has been extensively excavated by archaeologists and today, in the foundations of the temple of Zeus, the outline of the great statue's base is clearly visible. In addition, the ruins of Phidias's workshop were uncovered. We have some bronze tools, a few small terra-cotta molds for forming the folds of the golden robe, and some scraps of ivory. But most poignantly, a small bowl was found, made in the Athenian style, and on the bottom are scratched the words I BELONG TO PHIDIAS. It is the drinking cup of the most famous artist of the ancient world.

THE MAUSOLEUM AT HALICARNASSUS

Asia Minor was dominated by the vast Persian Empire. One of the Empire's provinces was the kingdom of Caria, whose capital was Halicarnassus, a bustling port on the Aegean Sea. The ruler of Caria, a vassal of the emperor of Persia, was King Mausolus. He ruled along with his wife, Artemisia, who was also his sister. Marriage between siblings was not an unusual practice in royal families in the Near East. Mausolus died in 353 B.C., and Artemisia in 351. Both were buried inside an immense and very elaborate stone tomb overlooking the harbor of Halicarnassus. It was known as the Mausoleum, a word that has come to refer to any large imposing official tomb.

We know a lot about the Mausoleum. The foundations have been excavated, so we know its scale; and when combined with descriptions from the ancient writers, we can imagine its general appearance. The structure was built in three levels. At the bottom was a lofty rectangular podium. On top of this were thirty-six columns arranged like the porch of a Greek temple, surrounding the central core of the structure. This colonnade supported the third stage, which was shaped like a pyramid. The tomb itself was a subterranean crypt. Altogether it was a very unusual design, part Persian, part Greek, part Egyptian. And it was huge, as tall as a fifteen-story building.

But the glory of the Mausoleum was its decoration. The building was practically encrusted with marble sculpture. There were several friezes—bands of relief sculpture that ran around the building. There were hundreds of figures carved fully in the round. Men and horses were arranged in scenes of battle, illustrating the stories of Greek mythology. Hunting scenes included scores of wild animals. There were many large standing figures, some almost twice life-size—perhaps portraits of Mausolus's ancestors. Crowning the entire edifice was the monumental ceremonial figure of Mausolus in a chariot pulled by four horses. The sculpture of the Mausoleum,

like all Greek sculpture, was brightly painted. The effect of the entire gigantic gleaming monument bristling with colorful sculpture was dazzling—a display of the wealth and power of the royal dynasty of Caria.

Greek writers tell us that five famous sculptors worked on the Mausoleum. Pythis made the chariot group on the summit. The other four artists each made the decoration for one side of the building: Scopas on the east, Bryaxis on the north, Timotheus on the south, and Leochares on the west. These sculptors were probably the designers, directing teams of assistants who actually did most of the carving. Since it has been estimated that it takes one man a year to carve a life-size figure, the labor spent in making the hundreds of figures on the Mausoleum was immense.

King Mausolus and Queen Artemisia rested undisturbed for 1,800 years while the great tomb gradually deteriorated above them. Earthquakes took their toll, and in the fifteenth century A.D., the ruined structure was used as a stone quarry for building a castle-fortress nearby. In 1522, the crypt was discovered and looted. Houses were eventually built over the site and it was lost.

The Mausoleum was rediscovered when the archaeologists realized that fragments of sculpture built into the walls of the nearby castle must have come from the famous tomb. Eventually the foundations were excavated, and more pieces of building blocks and broken fragments of sculpture were found. These fragments may be seen in museums today.

Ancient writers describe a podium, some columns, a pyramid, hundreds of sculpted figures of varying sizes, and five famous sculptors. What remains are thousands of fragments. Putting it all together and determining who did what and what went where is a fantastic puzzle that has intrigued generations of archaeologists. Every expert has a different opinion about exactly how the Mausoleum looked. Perhaps one of them is correct.

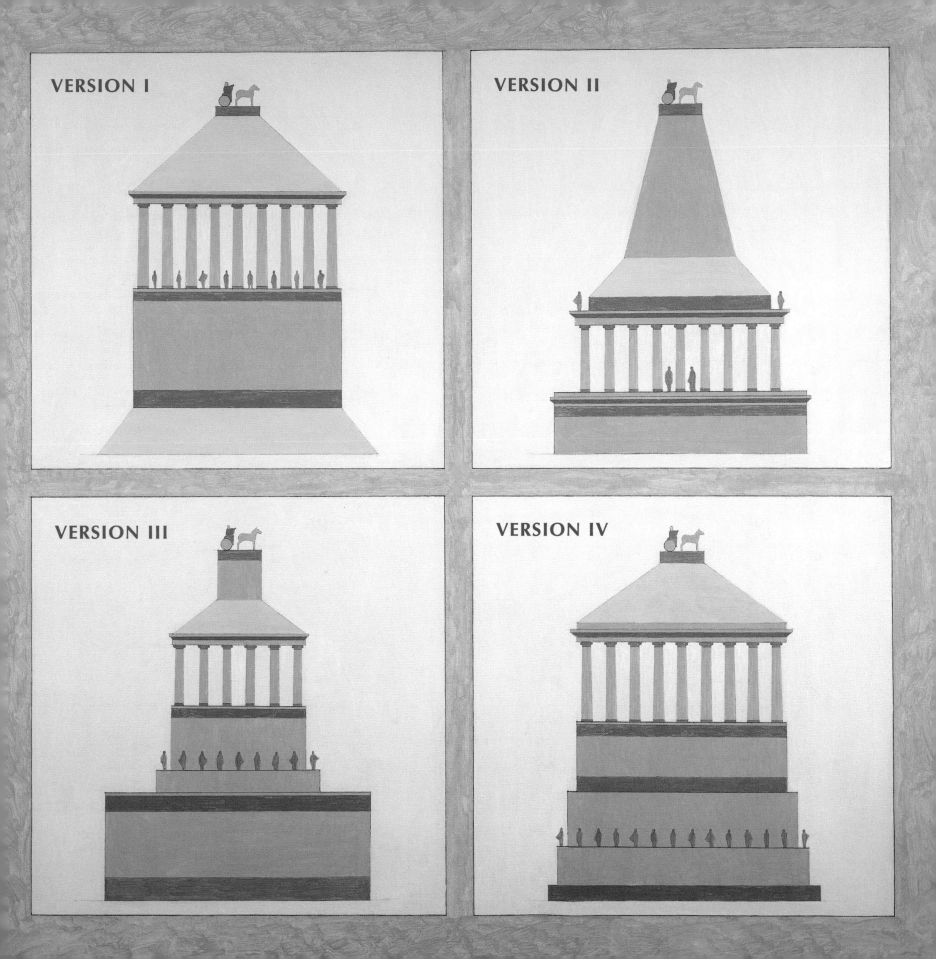

VERSION I

VERSION II

VERSION III

VERSION IV

THE COLOSSUS OF RHODES

Rhodes is a large island off the southern coast of Asia Minor. Its fields were fertile, its climate was mild, and its people were prosperous. They believed that their island was particularly blessed by the Greek sun god, Helios. But in 305 B.C., the island was invaded and the capital city, also called Rhodes, was placed under siege. The citizens of Rhodes fought so bravely to defend the city that eventually their enemy retreated and left the island, leaving behind all of their military equipment. According to legend, the Rhodians melted down all of the bronze weapons, shields, and war machinery to fashion a gigantic statue of Helios in thanks for their victory.

We know that the Colossus of Rhodes really existed. We know roughly how big it was and a little of how it was made, and we know how it disappeared, but that's about all. We do not know its pose or how it looked, or even exactly where it stood in the city of Rhodes.

The enormous statue was made in the years between 294 and 282 B.C. It was fashioned by the sculptor Chares of Lindos and stood about one hundred and ten feet tall. It was built from the ground up by casting the bronze in segments, one on top of the next. As the statue rose, it was weighted down and reinforced on the inside with blocks of stone and short iron bars. Earth was piled up around it ever higher to provide a working platform, and when the statue was complete, the earth was removed and Helios stood alone, the largest statue ever made in the ancient world.

In the sixteenth century Maerten van Heemskerck engraved his famous image of the Colossus straddling the harbor entrance of Rhodes with ships passing between his legs. For four hundred years this picture was taken to be true. But it is technically impossible. Helios was almost certainly shown as a nude young man, probably standing in a relaxed pose, which was the style of the time in sculpture. We are told that one arm was raised. But what does that mean? Was it raised above his head or just up to elbow height? Was Helios carrying anything? A torch perhaps, or a bow and

arrows to represent rays of sunlight? Maybe he had a robe draped over one arm, symbolizing the cloak of night. It seems likely that Helios had a crown of rays—he is sometimes shown that way in Greek art—but all of these are educated guesses. We must also guess about the statue's location. It could have stood at the harbor entrance, or perhaps it was in the sacred precinct near the temple of the god. Until archaeologists uncover the evidence, we simply do not know.

We do know that the Colossus of Rhodes stood for only about fifty-six years. In 226 B.C., it collapsed in a violent earthquake. We are told that it broke at the knees. But even in ruins it was an object of wonder. One ancient writer described it like this: "Few people can make their arms meet around the thumb of the figure, and the fingers are larger than most statues; and where the limbs have broken off enormous cavities yawn, while inside are seen great masses of rock with the weight of which the artist steadied it when he erected it."

The remains of the Colossus stayed in place where they fell for nearly a millennium. The Rhodians were told by an oracle not to rebuild the statue. Then in A.D. 654, Rhodes was conquered by Arabs, who broke up the fallen giant and sent the bronze to Syria. Legend says that it took nine hundred camels to transport the valuable metal. No doubt it was melted down and turned back into weapons, the fate of most bronze statues from the ancient world.

The word "colossus" has come to mean any particularly gigantic statue. Today we have our own colossus of the modern world. It stands in New York Harbor, an enormous metal figure larger even than the ancient statue of Helios. We call it the Statue of Liberty.

THE PHAROS AT ALEXANDRIA

The last of the Seven Wonders of the Ancient World was not a huge statue or a vast tomb or a grand temple. It was a building with a practical purpose. Alexandria was the Hellenistic capital of Egypt and the most important city of the age. Founded by Alexander the Great himself in 332 B.C., it was a new city that grew into a cosmopolitan center of trade and culture. It was famous for its great library, now lost, which was said to hold all of the knowledge of the ancient world. The reefs and shoals at the approach to Alexandria's busy harbor made it dangerous for ships to navigate. So on the rocky island of Pharos, at the harbor entrance, a gigantic tower was built to serve as a marker and a lighthouse. Named after the island, the Pharos had an inscription that read: SOSTRATUS THE CNIDIAN, FRIEND OF THE SOVEREIGNS, DEDICATED THIS, FOR THE SAFETY OF THOSE WHO SAIL THE SEAS. Sostratus was probably a wealthy nobleman from the island of Cnidos, who paid for the structure. The lighthouse was finished by about 250 B.C.

The Pharos was an amazing technical triumph—one of the greatest feats of engineering in the ancient world. The Great Pyramid stands today because it is completely stable. With its broad base and tapering sides, it can erode, but it won't collapse. But the Pharos was a hollow building with large interior spaces. It was designed and engineered, with an internal structure of stone and heavy timbers, to stand upright. In this, its engineers were very successful. It stood for nearly fifteen hundred years. After the pyramids, the Pharos was the tallest structure built in the ancient world.

We have a very good idea of how the Pharos looked. Its image is found on many ancient coins made in Alexandria. The lighthouse rose in three stages above a low, broad platform built on the rocks of Pharos Island. The lowest stage was square, the second was octagonal, and the top was cylindrical. At its peak was a bronze statue of Zeus, three hundred and eighty feet above the waves.

The Pharos was nearly the height of a forty-story skyscraper. Our best description of the enormous tower comes from an Arab traveler who visited it in the year A.D. 1166, before it fell into ruins. He tells us that there was no stairway in the lower section, but a spiraling ramp that gradually ascended around the cylindrical core of the building. When he saw it, the upper stage of the Pharos had been turned into a small mosque, but in the past it held the lighting apparatus. We are not sure precisely how this worked, but it was probably an array of highly polished bronze sheets, which could be arranged to reflect the light of a small bonfire. We cannot be sure of the fuel. Wood was scarce and very expensive in Egypt. But perhaps it was imported specifically for the Pharos's light. Or maybe they burned oil or even animal dung instead. It has also been suggested that the Pharos may have served as a heliograph, a device for sending messages by reflected sunlight.

Used as a working lighthouse for centuries, the Pharos tumbled into the harbor of Alexandria during an earthquake sometime between A.D. 1303 and 1349. In the fifteenth century a great Islamic fort was built on its site, using some of the stones from its ruins. The Pharos was the first building to be designed as a lighthouse, and its echo can be seen in hundreds of lighthouses all over the world. Its name also survives as the word for "lighthouse" in many languages (*faro* in Italian and Spanish; *phare* in French). Engineers did not attempt to construct such a tall building again for many centuries.

In the 1990s, underwater archaeologists began exploring the ancient harbor of Alexandria. There, only twenty-five feet down, they found thousands of stone blocks from the Pharos, lying right where they fell. They raised from the seabed fragments of six huge granite statues that stood originally at the base of the great lighthouse. They are official portraits of the Hellenistic kings and queens of Alexandria, in the traditional ritual costume of the ancient Egyptian pharaohs, exactly like that worn by Khufu during the age of the pyramids more than two thousand years before.

The traditional Seven Wonders were not the only spectacular structures of the ancient world. There was the temple of Amon-Ra at Karnak in Egypt, the largest religious edifice ever built. In Greece, Athens had its magnificent Parthenon, considered by many to be the most beautiful building in the world. The Romans built the Colosseum, a gigantic arena that could hold fifty thousand people. They constructed aqueducts hundreds of miles long to bring water to their capital city, and a road system that linked the entire Mediterranean world.

Other civilizations have made wonders of their own. China has its Great Wall, the only man-made structure on Earth that can be easily seen from space. In India, there is the exquisite Taj Mahal, which rivals the Parthenon in beauty. The Aztecs and Maya of Central America constructed immense ceremonial centers with huge pyramid-temples. The Incas built the lofty mountain citadel of Machu Picchu. In medieval Europe, people built fantastic gothic cathedrals, and later, during the Renaissance, they erected great domed buildings, such as Saint Peter's Basilica in Rome.

In the modern age, we have our own monuments: towering skyscrapers, tremendous bridges and dams, great highway systems, as well as vast power and communications networks. We have even learned to fly, and now, at the dawn of the third millennium A.D., forty-five centuries after the age of the pyramids, we stand on the brink of the age of space. No one knows what wonders the future will bring. But we do know this: The civilizations that made the Seven Wonders of the Ancient World are gone, and one day our civilization will vanish as well. We will become a period in history, like the Hellenistic age. Perhaps many centuries from now, in the far distant future, archaeologists will uncover the ruins of the marvels of our own modern age and they will wonder about the people who made them—us.

SEVEN WONDERS OF THE ANCIENT WORLD
and some modern marvels, all shown to scale

U. S. Capitol   **Statue of Liberty**   **Colossus of Rhodes**   **Statue of Zeus**

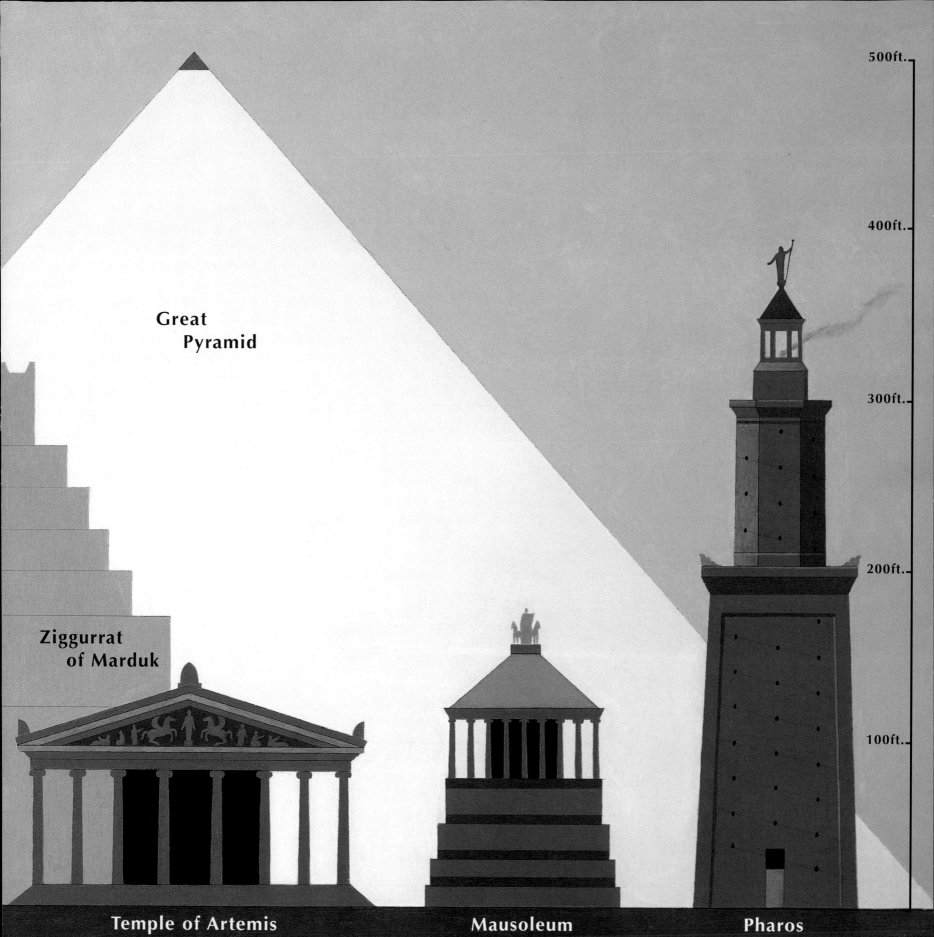

Great
Pyramid

Ziggurrat
of Marduk

500ft.

400ft.

300ft.

200ft.

100ft.

Temple of Artemis   Mausoleum   Pharos

For Nick

Atheneum Books for Young Readers

An imprint of Simon & Schuster Children's Publishing Division

1230 Avenue of the Americas

New York, New York 10020

Copyright © 2002 by Lynn Curlee

All rights reserved, including the right of reproduction in whole or in part in any form.

Book design by Abelardo Martínez and Kristen Smith

The text of this book is set in Deepdene H.

The illustrations are rendered in acrylic on canvas.

Mr. Curlee would like to thank Ed Peterson for photographing the paintings.

Printed in Hong Kong

2 4 6 8 10 9 7 5 3

Library of Congress Cataloging-in-Publication Data

Curlee, Lynn.

Seven wonders of the ancient world / by Lynn Curlee.

p.   cm.

ISBN 0-689-83182-X

1. Seven Wonders of the World—Juvenile literature.

[1. Seven Wonders of the World.] I. Title.

N533 .C88 2002

709'.01—dc21   00-046919